WHISPERS OF LOVE IN THE WIND

TUSHAR RAJ

To the love of my life, who has been my constant companion, my source of happiness, and my reason to smile every day. You have shown me what true love really is and have helped me discover myself in ways I never thought possible. Thank you for being there for me, through thick and thin, for supporting me in my dreams, and for being my everything.

This book is dedicated to you, my love. Your unwavering love, kindness, and understanding have inspired me to write this story, and I hope it brings a smile to your face every time you read it. I am so grateful for the journey we have shared, and I am looking forward to the many adventures that lie ahead.

Thank you for being the reason I wake up each day with a smile on my face and a heart overflowing with love. You are my everything, and I am so blessed to have you in my life. This book is a testament to our love, and I am proud to share it with the world.

With love,

Tushar Raj

Contents

Foreword

Love is a magical thing. It has the power to transform our lives, bring us joy and happiness, and fill us with hope and inspiration. It's a journey that we all embark on at some point in our lives, and it's one that we never forget.

This book is a tribute to that journey, a celebration of love in all its forms. It's a story of two people who found each other in the unlikeliest of places, and who were drawn together by a force greater than themselves. It's a tale of two hearts beating as one, and of two souls entwined in a love that would last a lifetime.

As you read this book, you'll experience the ups and downs of love, the laughter and the tears, and the joys and the challenges. You'll be transported to a world where anything is possible, where love is all that matters, and where two hearts can conquer the world.

So sit back, relax, and let the wind carry you away on a journey of love and romance. This is a story of hope, courage, and of love, and it's a story that will stay with you long after you've finished reading. So take a deep breath, and let the whispers of love carry you away.

Acknowledgements

I would like to express my deepest gratitude to all the people who have helped me bring this book to life. First and foremost, I would like to thank my family for their unwavering support and encouragement. Their love and understanding have been my greatest strength throughout this journey.

I would also like to thank my editor, who helped me refine my writing and bring the story to its full potential. Your insights and suggestions were invaluable, and I am grateful for your guidance.

A special thank you goes out to my friends, who have always been there to lend a listening ear and offer encouragement. Your belief in me has meant the world.

I would also like to express my gratitude to all the readers who have taken the time to read this book. Your feedback and support have been a source of inspiration and motivation, and I am truly grateful for each and every one of you.

Finally, I would like to acknowledge the power of love, which has inspired me to write this book. Love has the power to change lives, and it is my hope that this book will bring joy and inspiration to those who read it.

Thank you to all who have been a part of this journey, and I hope you will continue to join me on future adventures.

With love and gratitude,
Tushar Raj

Prologue

In a world filled with chaos and uncertainty, there is love that stands the test of time. It is a love that speaks to us in the gentle whispers of the wind, reminding us that there is still hope, still joy, still happiness. It is a love that brings us together, binding our hearts and our souls, and filling our lives with a light that shines brighter than the sun.

This is a love story unlike any other. A story of two people who found each other against all odds, and held on to their love with all their hearts. A story of the power of love, and how it can change our lives forever. A story of a love that will stand the test of time, and be remembered for generations to come.

So let us journey together, into the world of whispers and dreams, where love reigns supreme, and the wind speaks its secrets. This is a love story that will take us on a journey of laughter and tears, of happiness and heartbreak, and of two hearts beating as one. This is the story of "Whispers of Love in the Wind."

Preface

Love is a magical thing. It can change our lives, and our outlook on the world, and bring us joy beyond measure. This is the story of two people who found love in the most unexpected of places. It's a tale of love, adventure, and the power of fate.

In a world where people are so focused on themselves, it's rare to find love that truly changes everything. But that's exactly what happened when two strangers met in a park one day. It was a chance encounter that changed their lives forever.

"Whispers of Love in the Wind" is a story about two people who found love in a world where it can be hard to find. It's about the joy of discovering someone who truly understands you and the happiness of sharing your life with someone who makes everything better.

So sit back, relax, and let the winds of love carry you away in this enchanting tale. This is a story about the power of love and the magic it brings into our lives. It's a story about two people who found each other and never let go.

CHAPTER ONE

The Beginning of a New Love

It all started on a sunny day in the park. The birds chirped and the wind blew gently through the trees. That's where she first saw him, sitting on a bench, lost in thought. She couldn't help but be drawn to him, his eyes sparkling like diamonds in the sunlight. As she walked by, she couldn't help but catch his gaze. It was as if the world around them had stopped, and all that remained was the two of them.

At that moment, she knew that this was the beginning of something special. She felt a spark within her that she had never felt before, and she knew that this was just the start of a love that would change her life forever. She felt a rush of excitement as if a whole new world was opening up before her.

As she continued to walk, she couldn't help but think about him. Who was he? What did he like? What was he thinking? She felt as if she had known him for a lifetime, and yet, she had never seen him before.

Days passed, and she couldn't get him out of her mind. She found herself walking by the park every day, hoping to see him again. And one day, there he was, sitting on the same bench as before. This time, she mustered up the courage to go talk to him.

As she approached him, he looked up, and a smile spread across his face. They talked for hours, about everything and anything. They laughed and shared their hopes and dreams. They both felt a deep connection, and they knew that this was the start of something truly special.

From that day on, they were inseparable. They went on adventures, trying new things and exploring the world together. They shared their lives, their hopes, and fears, and they grew to love each other more and more with each passing day.

This was the beginning of a new love, a love that would last a lifetime. They knew that they had found something special, and they were grateful for each other, every day. And as the wind whispered their names, they held each other close, knowing that this was just the start of a beautiful journey together.

Two Hearts Beating as One

Their hearts beat in unison as they stood hand in hand, staring deeply into each other's eyes. They had finally found their soulmates, and the feeling was indescribable. They could feel the love radiating from each other's hearts, and it was as if their souls were intertwined. They felt whole, complete and more alive than ever before.

"I love you," he whispered, as he leaned in for a kiss. The kiss was filled with love, passion and a promise of a future together. They knew that from this moment on, they would face the world together, side by side, as they embarked on a journey of love and happiness.

As they walked through the fields, the wind whispered their names, as if it was endorsing their love. They felt as if they were the only two people in the world, and that their love was unbreakable. They talked about their hopes and dreams for the future, and they both knew that they could make anything happen as long as they had each other.

"I never thought I would find someone like you," she said with a smile. "You complete me in a way I never thought possible." He looked at her with a twinkle in his eye, and replied, "I feel the same way, my love. You are the missing piece of my heart, and I will love you forever."

As they continued on their walk, they could feel the love between them growing stronger by the second. They knew that they had each other to rely on, no matter what life threw their way. They were two hearts beating as one, and nothing could ever break the bond they shared.

They held each other tightly, knowing that they had found the love of a lifetime. The wind whispered sweet nothings in their ears, and they knew that their love would only grow stronger with each passing day. They were two hearts beating as one, and they would never let go.

CHAPTER THREE

The Wind Whispers Your Name

It was a warm summer day when Sarah walked through the park, feeling the sun on her skin and the wind in her hair. She took a deep breath, feeling content and at peace when suddenly she heard something that made her heart skip a beat. A voice, soft and gentle, whispered her name in the wind. She looked around, but nobody was there. She shrugged it off, thinking she was just imagining things, but the voice came again.

"Sarah," it said, a little louder this time.

She felt a shiver run down her spine. It was the most beautiful sound she had ever heard, and it seemed to be calling to her. She followed the voice, and it led her to a bench in a quiet corner of the park. She sat down, and the voice came again, a little clearer this time.

"Sarah, my love," it said.

She looked around again, but still, nobody was there. She was starting to get worried, but the voice was so warm and inviting, she couldn't help but feel drawn to it. And then, as if by magic, she saw a figure in the distance, walking towards her. It was Jack, the man she had been seeing for the past few weeks. He smiled at her, and she felt her heart soar.

"Did you hear it too?" she asked, as he took a seat next to her.

"Hear what?" he replied.

"The voice. It whispered my name," she said, feeling a little silly.

"Ah, that," Jack said, with a smile. "That was me. I've been trying to find a way to get your attention."

Sarah's eyes went wide. She had never felt so surprised and happy at the same time. Jack took her hand and looked into her eyes.

"I love you, Sarah. The wind whispers your name because it knows how much I love you," he said and leaned in for a kiss.

And as they kissed, surrounded by the warm sun and the gentle breeze, Sarah knew that she had found the love of her life. The wind had whispered her name, and she would always remember that moment as the beginning of their story.

CHAPTER FOUR

A Love Story to Remember

It was a beautiful day in the city of Paris. The sun was shining, the birds were singing, and there was a light breeze blowing. Emma and Jack were taking a walk in the park, hand in hand. They were both so in love and they could feel it in the air.

"I never thought I would find someone like you, Jack," Emma said as they walked through the lush greenery.

"Same here, Emma. You're my everything," Jack replied as he squeezed her hand.

As they walked, they talked about their dreams and aspirations. They talked about their families, their favorite movies, and their favorite books. They laughed and smiled, and before they knew it, hours had passed.

Finally, they reached the bench where they had shared their first kiss. They sat down and looked at each other, both feeling grateful for the love they had found.

"I never knew love could feel this good," Emma said as she leaned her head on Jack's shoulder.

"Me either, Em. I'm so lucky to have you in my life," Jack replied as he put his arm around her.

They sat there for a while, just enjoying the peacefulness of the moment. They talked about how they had met and how their love had grown. They talked about their future and all the amazing things they wanted to do together.

"I want to make sure this love story is one that we'll always remember," Jack said as he looked into Emma's eyes.

"Me too, Jack. You're my everything and I want to hold on to this love forever," Emma replied as she leaned in for a kiss.

And with that, they sealed their love with a kiss. It was a love story that they would always remember, a love story that would be told for generations to come. A love story that would always be remembered as the epitome of true love and happiness.

CHAPTER FIVE

The Magic of Our Connection

It was a warm summer night and Jack and Emma were lying in the grass, looking up at the stars. They were both lost in thought, feeling the strong connection that they shared.

"Do you ever stop and think about how amazing it is that we found each other?" Jack said as he held Emma's hand.

"All the time," Emma replied as she looked into Jack's eyes. "It's like fate brought us together."

They talked about all the moments that led up to their meeting. They talked about the jobs they had, the friends they had, and the coincidences that brought them together.

"It's like we were meant to be," Emma said as she smiled.

"I know," Jack replied as he leaned in for a kiss.

As they lay there, they talked about all the things they wanted to do together. They talked about traveling the world, trying new foods, and experiencing new adventures. They talked about starting a family and growing old together.

"We have a special connection, Emma. A connection that not many people have," Jack said as he held her close.

"I know, Jack. And I'm so grateful for it. I'm grateful for you," Emma replied as she looked up at the stars.

They lay there for a while longer, feeling the magic of their connection. They both knew that they had found something special and they never wanted to let it go.

"I love you, Jack," Emma said as she snuggled into his arms.

"I love you too, Em," Jack replied as he held her close.

The magic of their connection was undeniable. It was a love that would last a lifetime and they both knew it. It was a love that would always be remembered and cherished. The magic of their connection was a love story to be remembered.

CHAPTER SIX

Finding Happiness in Each Other's Arms

It was a warm summer night and Jack and Emma were lying on a blanket in the park, looking up at the stars. They had been together for a year now, and their love for each other had only grown stronger.

"Emma, I just want you to know how much you mean to me," Jack said as he held her close. "You make me the happiest man in the world."

"And you make me the happiest woman, Jack. I never thought I would find someone who loves me as much as you do," Emma replied as she snuggled closer to him.

They talked about their future and all the things they wanted to do together. They talked about their dreams and their hopes. They talked about their families and how they wanted to make them proud.

"I just want to make sure we're always happy, Em. I want to make sure we're always there for each other," Jack said as he looked into her eyes.

"Me too, Jack. That's all I want, just to be with you and be happy," Emma replied as she leaned in for a kiss.

They held each other close, finding happiness in each other's arms. It was a moment they would always cherish, a moment of pure bliss and joy. They knew that as long as they had each other, they could conquer anything.

And as they lay there, surrounded by the stars and the peacefulness of the night, they knew that they had found something truly special. They had found happiness, love, and a bond that would never be broken. They were truly grateful for each other and for the love they shared.

CHAPTER SEVEN

Sharing Moments of Bliss

Emma and Jack's love for each other continued to grow stronger every day. They spent every moment they could together, creating memories that would last a lifetime.

One day, Jack took Emma on a surprise picnic in the park. He had packed a basket of her favorite foods and drinks, along with a beautiful bouquet of flowers. They found a quiet spot under a tree and set up their blanket.

"This is so sweet, Jack," Emma said as she gazed at the picnic spread in front of them.

"I just wanted to make this day special for you, Em," Jack replied with a smile.

They spent the whole day talking and laughing, enjoying each other's company. They talked about their favorite childhood memories, their hopes and dreams, and all the things they were grateful for in their lives.

As they were eating, Jack pulled out a small box from his pocket. He got down on one knee and opened the box, revealing a beautiful diamond ring.

"Emma, I love you more than anything in this world. Will you marry me?" Jack said, his eyes shining with love.

Emma's heart skipped a beat as she looked into Jack's eyes. She felt like the luckiest person in the world to have found such amazing love.

"Yes, Jack. I will marry you," she said as she threw her arms around his neck and gave him a kiss.

From that day forward, they were inseparable. They spent every moment they could together, sharing moments of bliss and creating memories that they would treasure forever. They knew that they were meant to be together and they were grateful for the love they had found.

As they lay on the blanket, looking up at the sky, they felt so grateful for the love they shared. They were living a love story that would be remembered for generations to come, and they were both so grateful for each other.

CHAPTER EIGHT

Forever in Love

The sun was setting over the horizon, casting a warm golden glow over the city of Paris. Jack and Emma were standing on the balcony of their apartment, looking out at the view. They had been married for five years and their love for each other was just as strong as it was on the day they met.

"Do you remember the day we got married?" Jack asked as he wrapped his arms around Emma.

"Of course I do, Jack. It was the best day of my life," Emma replied as she snuggled into his embrace.

They reminisced about their wedding day, how beautiful it was, and how happy they felt. They talked about their honeymoon and all the amazing places they had visited. They laughed about all the silly things they did and all the adventures they had.

"I never knew love could be this good," Emma said as she looked up at Jack.

"Me neither, Em. I'm so grateful for every day that I get to spend with you," Jack replied as he leaned in for a kiss.

They shared a sweet, tender kiss, a kiss that was filled with love and affection. They held each other tightly, their hearts beating as one.

"I promise to love you forever, Jack," Emma said as she looked into his eyes.

"And I promise to love you forever, Em. You're my everything," Jack replied as he hugged her even tighter.

They stood there, watching the sun set over the city, feeling so in love and so grateful for each other. They knew that their love would last forever, that they would always be together, no matter what. They were forever in love and that was all that mattered.

CHAPTER NINE

The Sweet Serenade of Love

It was a warm summer evening and Emma and Jack were sitting on their balcony, enjoying the cool breeze. The stars were shining bright in the sky and a gentle melody was playing in the background. Jack had brought out his guitar and was strumming a beautiful tune.

"What's this song, Jack?" Emma asked, her eyes sparkling with delight.

"It's a song I wrote for you, my love," Jack replied, a soft smile spreading across his face.

Emma felt a flutter in her heart as she listened to Jack's beautiful voice singing the words he had written just for her. The lyrics were full of love, devotion, and admiration. They spoke of the love they shared and how they were meant to be together forever.

As the song came to an end, Jack put down his guitar and took Emma's hand. "I love you, Emma. You're the one I want to spend the rest of my life with," he said, his eyes filled with warmth and affection.

"I love you too, Jack. You're the one who makes my life complete," Emma replied, her heart overflowing with joy and happiness.

They sat there for a while, just enjoying each other's company and the peace of the evening. They talked about their dreams and the future they wanted to build together. They talked about their hopes and the adventures they wanted to embark on.

As they watched the stars twinkling in the sky, they both knew that they were in the right place, with the right person. They were meant to be together, forever and always. The sweet serenade of love had brought them together and they were never going to let go.

From that moment on, the sweet serenade of love would always be a reminder of the love they shared and the beautiful memories they had created. It would always be a special part of their love story and a symbol of the happiness and joy they felt every day.

Together, Against the Wind

It had been several years since Emma and Jack had first fallen in love in the park in Paris. They had been through many ups and downs together, but their love had only grown stronger with each passing day. They were each other's rock, and they never gave up on each other.

One day, they found themselves facing a new challenge. A strong wind was blowing and it seemed like nothing was going their way. Jack was feeling overwhelmed and Emma was feeling stressed. But they both knew that they could face anything as long as they had each other.

"Jack, we can get through this together," Emma said as she put her hand on his shoulder.

"I know, Em. We always do," Jack replied as he looked into her eyes.

They held hands and walked together against the wind. They talked about their worries and their fears. They talked about their love and how much they meant to each other. And as they talked, the wind slowly began to calm down.

"You know what, Em? I think we're going to be okay," Jack said as he smiled at her.

"I know we will, Jack. We have each other, and that's all that matters," Emma replied as she leaned in for a kiss.

They reached the end of the park and the wind had completely stopped. The sun was shining again and the birds were singing. They stood there, hand in hand, and looked out at the beautiful view.

"I love you, Jack," Emma said as she looked into his eyes.

"I love you too, Em. Forever and always," Jack replied as he hugged her.

And with that, they walked away together, ready to face whatever challenges lay ahead. Because they knew that as long as they had each other, they could conquer anything. Their love was a love story to remember, a love story that would always be remembered as a shining example of true love and devotion.